Light reading

What's cooking?

written and illustrated by John Light

Published by Child's Play (International) Ltd

Swindon   **Bologna**   **New York**

© M. Twinn 1989   ISBN 0-85953-337-9   Printed in Singapore

Library of Congress Catalogue Number 90-34355
This impression 1992

Nanna is a really good cook. On her birthday
she makes sausages, jelly and chocolate cookies.

Mum is a good cook, too,
and makes a lot of dirty dishes for Dad.

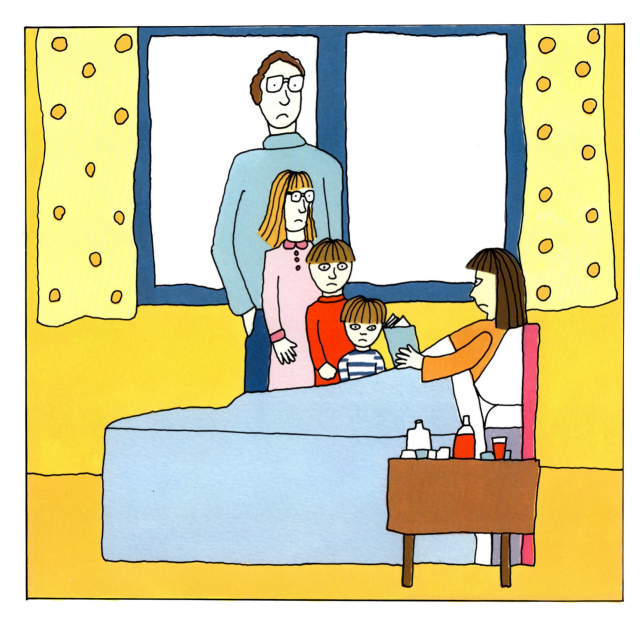

Sometimes she is ill and has to stay in bed.

When that happens, Dad does the cooking...

... and everyone feels ill.

So Mark and Roger decided
they had better learn to cook properly...

... like Uncle Richard. He has to be good at cooking because he lives with his cat...

... who is very hard to please.

Roger dreams about apple pies.

The dangerous part of making apple pies
is catching the apples...

Especially for the one below.

Mark laughed so much, he fell off his branch.

"Perhaps bananas would be safer," said Roger.

Mum showed them how to make meringues.
"First, you need a big apron," she said.

"Separating the egg white is difficult," said Mum.

"It's important to leave enough in the bowls
to scrape out," said Mark.

Mark baked a cake.
He listened to see if it was cooked.

Mark decorated the cake.

Roger iced some cakes.
But he put in too much colouring.

"I've got a headache in my tummy," Roger moaned.

When Mum is tired, Katherine sometimes cooks.

"Have some jelly," she said, pouring it into Mark's plate.

"I don't like custard," said Roger,
but Katherine didn't notice.